DOSES:
LOVE & FRIENDSHIP IN VIBRANT PIECES

TY SCOTT KING

DOSES:
LOVE & FRIENDSHIP IN VIBRANT PIECES

DOSES

God, thank you for being the very foundation of love.

Mike, thank you for making romance
easy to write about.

Mom, your absence has proven to me
that love outlasts the grave.

Dad, I love our love.

Pop, thank you for holding my hand.

Siblings, thank you all for being my
first and most faithful friends.

Friends, thank you all for tolerating my quirks and
cheering me on every time I say, "I've got an idea!"

"Love is more important than anything else.
It is what ties everything completely together."
—Colossians 3:14

TABLE OF CONTENTS

"So encourage each other
and build each other up …."
—1 Thessalonians 5:11

NOTHING MAKES THE DEVIL MADDER

Their conversations always seemed to start with laughter. And not just chuckles either, but full-on belly-aching, tear-jerking laughter. Throughout the years, these women had become masterful at reading through each other's snickers and giggles just as well as they could decipher pain in unspoken words. And considering how they met, it could only have been God who allowed their friendship to blossom into such a profound sisterhood.

∞

SEVEN YEARS EARLIER

Raquell

Raquell was head over heels in love with Collin. She had long ago come to grips with the fact that he wasn't tall, dark, and handsome like nearly all the men she'd dated previously. But he more than made up for his looks with the ability he had to keep a smile on her face. Raquell was willing to bet that Collin had talked the fairytale Prince out of almost all of his charm because he had tons of it. As a matter of fact, his larger-than-life personality was the culprit behind Raquell's countless sleepless nights.

"I'm just making new friends," Collin would tell Raquell whenever she caught him flirting with other women.

And her response was always the same: "Nobody with a girlfriend needs that many female friends."

"You're just overreacting, El," he would retort. "I'm not like those other men you dated. I know how to be faithful."

"Yes, I'm sure you do," Raquell would say while trying not to let her annoyance pierce through her tone. "Just not to me," she always wanted to add.

But she never said it because after years of dealing with this man, she knew that whether she scolded, begged, or pleaded it would all be to no avail. Collin wouldn't stop cheating and the even harsher truth was that she wouldn't let him go. They were a dangerous pair—him reckless and her desperate.

Raquell knew the adage, "There are more fish in the sea" was true, but she didn't have enough time to catch another fish. This one, as slimy as he was, would have to do. So, she put up with Collin because she wanted a man and a baby before it was too late. After all, she was knocking on forty-seven and needed a bun in her oven sooner than later.

∞

Constance

After spending hours in her closet and trying on practically everything she owned, Constance came to the same conclusion she had already drawn a thousand times—she had nothing appropriate to wear. Her desperation mounting, she looked at the pile of clothes flung across her bed and the assorted high heels strewn all over her carpeted bedroom floor and erupted into tears. She couldn't believe that she had finally gotten the call to interview for the position of district representative and her wardrobe would be her downfall. Not knowing what else to do, she picked up the phone to call her sister. It barely rang once before it went to voicemail.

"She's got some nerve sending me to voicemail," Constance muttered. "After all I've done for that brat."

Yet, as livid as she was that her sister was dodging her, Constance knew that Nora was her only hope at getting the money she needed to buy something that would keep her from having to go to this interview looking two-steps from homeless—which actually wasn't too far from the truth. After all, Constance's harsh reality was that she had gotten herself into a bind when she left her job.

Admittedly, being an editorial writer for one of the most widely read magazines in the country had more than paid her bills, but she was tired of doing work she wasn't passionate about. What fueled her fire was politics. So, she took a leap of faith and quit without the safety net of having another position lined up. Now finally—after six months of dead-end leads and piled up debt—the call came for this interview, and she was determined to look her best.

Shooting a frantic glance at the vintage clock that hung over the frame of her bedroom door, Constance calculated that if she left within the next five minutes she could make it to Nora's, borrow some cash, and get to the mall with time to spare.

∞

Raquell

"Are you canceling our lunch date again, Collin? Because to me that's what it sounds like," Raquell whined into her Bluetooth while weaving in and out of traffic.

"You're hearing me wrong, El," Collin replied. I'm not canceling. I'm postponing."

Sighing heavily over Collin's attempt to make her think she was an idiot who had no understanding of the difference between canceling and postponing, Raquell tried to insert logic into the conversation.

"Babe, I'm already on my way. As a matter of fact, I'll be there in less than ten minutes."

"I understand, El, but you know I had to fire my last assistant after only three days. I've got to look over this applicants' resume before I interview her."

Tempted to say, "I told you not to hire looks over integrity," Raquell bit her tongue and let Collin continue his rant.

The more he yapped, the angrier she got. First of all, she hated it when he called her El. She had always hated it. And she was sure that she had told him that. But, in typical Collin fashion he didn't listen. Second of all, she had a sneaking suspicion that Collin didn't give two craps about looking over that resume. She had come to know the way his mind worked, and she gathered that he was far more interested in finding out what physical assets this woman would bring to the table.

∞

Constance

It had taken some coaxing, but Nora came through for her and Constance was able to snag the perfect suit off the rack right before the mall closed. The next morning, she glided into her interview with all the faith in the world that the position would be hers.

"Thank you for taking the time out of your hectic schedule to personally interview me, Mr. Moore," she said while firmly shaking hands with the gentleman who greeted her in the entryway.

As they walked into his expansive office, he gestured toward a tan sofa in the corner and responded, "You're welcome, Ms. Hamilton. Have a seat."

Constance thought it was a bit strange that he didn't offer her the chair in front of his massive oak desk. Not wanting to come across as difficult, she took a seat on the edge of the plush sofa, positioned her attaché case on her lap, and crossed her legs at the ankles.

"So, tell me about your qualifications," Mr. Moore said while looking down at her resume.

"To summarize," Constance began shakily.

Then, after clearing her throat while reminding herself that she'd worked hard for this opportunity, she delved headfirst into a speech worthy of a Pulitzer Prize.

"Quite impressive," Mr. Moore responded while standing. "That leaves me with no further questions. Thank you for your time, Ms. Hamilton. We will be in touch."

Following his lead, Constance stood, shook his hand, and responded, "Thank you again for your time as well, Mr. Moore. I look forward to hearing from you soon."

Walking out of his office and down the hallway, Constance felt like lasers were on her backside. Instead of turning around, though, her gaze was fixed on the woman headed toward her whose eyes were ablaze with fury. As they eased past one another in the tight corridor, Constance recalled her own days of being with a trifling, crane-necked man, so she sent up a prayer for this ticked off girlfriend, wife, or whoever she was.

∞

Raquell

"I hope you had a good enough look to last a lifetime!" Raquell snapped at Collin as she bumped his shoulder with hers on the way into his office.

"El, what are you talking about?" he asked with a fake I'm-so-happy-to-see-you smile plastered on his face.

As Raquell stared through him like she had the superpower of burrowing through objects, she decided that she couldn't bear to waste a single breath on what was guaranteed to be another dead-end argument. Plus, she loathed eating alone.

So, she swallowed more of her self-respect and said, "I'm hungry. We should go eat."

∞

Constance and Raquell

"Eggs. Milk. Bread …"

Constance stood in the middle of the frozen foods aisle reviewing her grocery list to make sure that she didn't miss anything. Once she was satisfied that she had it all, she steered her over-loaded cart toward the checkout registers at the front of the store. Savings Village could be her best and worst friend all in the same day because of their incredibly low prices but miserably long lines, so Constance braced herself for the lengthy wait by grabbing one of her guilty pleasure magazines from the rack. As she thumbed through the pages, she marveled at the fact that most of the people she was reading about were famous for doing absolutely nothing of significance.

"Must be nice," she said aloud to herself with a giggle.

"What's that?" the silver-haired woman behind her asked.

"I'm sorry?" Constance responded.

"You said, 'Must be nice.' I was just wondering what you were talking about."

"Oh," Constance said while laughing. "I was just thinking that it must be nice to be famous for doing nothing."

"You got that right!" the woman replied enthusiastically.

This time they both let out a hearty laugh.

As their chuckling came to an end, a woman approached Constance's silver-haired snickering partner and asked, "Is this the butter you wanted, Mom?"

∞

It hadn't taken Constance very long to push that ghastly hallway episode with Mr. Moore and his woman out of her mind because just two days after that fiasco, she received a call, had an interview, and landed a position working for a respectable and happily married congressman. But she had wondered what happened to the woman with the fire in her eyes. And now, here she stood.

Not one to mince words, Constance came right out and said, "I remember you. Did you give ole Romeo Roaming Eyes a piece of your mind that day or what?"

Raquell was caught off guard by the direct question, plus it took her a minute to place the face attached to the inquiry. Then, a lightbulb went off in her head as she recalled where she had seen this woman before—Collin's office.

"Romeo Roaming Eyes," Raquell repeated back amused.

"I was going to call him something else, but I didn't want to offend anyone," Constance responded as her eyes darted to the silver-haired woman who had been standing aside quietly taking in their conversation.

"Never mind me," she said waving her hand at Constance. "I been around a long time. I've heard it all."

"Probably too much," Raquell responded jokingly as she stretched her hand out toward Constance. "By the way, I'm Raquell and this is my mom."

"Nice to meet you both. I'm Constance. Now, don't leave me hanging. I'm dying to know what happened!"

"Well," Raquell began, "the truth is Collin definitely had his faults, but I had mine too. So, I stuck around longer than I should have. Then, one day it hit me—I'd lost the confident woman I used to be, and I had to find her. So, I packed up my stuff and moved out. It's been tough, but I'm making it."

"Good for you!" Constance shouted.

A couple of people turned their heads and gave her annoyed looks like they were in a library instead of a bustling grocery store, but she didn't care. She was going to celebrate Raquell. Women didn't do enough of that these days.

With a satisfied smile, Raquell's mom said, "Jealousy could have reared its ugly head, but I'm glad you two didn't let that happen. Now, go on ahead and exchange numbers because y'all are meant to be sister-friends. Plus, nothing makes the devil madder than when he tries to divide us with foolishness, but we unite instead."

PLAY IT BY EAR

Janette could barely hear herself think over the extremely loud music seeping through the paper-thin walls of her apartment. She would be willing to swear under oath that she had asked her neighbor at least thirty times in the same amount of days if he could keep the music down after 9:00 p.m. Yet, here it was 10:30 at night and he was still letting his speakers blare electric guitar riffs as though the band was in his house performing a concert just for him.

She couldn't believe how inconsiderate he was being! Not only to her, but to their ninety-two-year-old upstairs neighbor, Mr. Klein. After working hard all his life, Janette was positive Mr. Klein wanted some peace and quiet just like her. But, come to think of it, Mr. Klein was losing his hearing, so the music probably didn't sound loud to him at all. In fact, depending on whether he had his hearing aids in or not, there was a huge chance he heard nothing at all. If only she could be so lucky!

Unable to put up with another minute of this mess, Janette was left with no choice but to pay yet another visit to her neighbor. He was lucky she didn't just call the police and have him cited for disturbing the peace.

She hadn't changed out of her sweats since her trip to the gym after work, but she had taken off her bra and she had no plans to put that contraption back on! So, to cover up her "girls," she grabbed her white and blue terry-cloth robe (that had seen far better days) and tugged the belt tight around her waist.

Trying not to be self-conscious about the fact that she'd put on a few pounds since her breakup with Todd, Janette looked herself over in her full-length bathroom mirror and concluded that she looked decent enough to go next door and give her highly inconsiderate neighbor a piece of her mind.

Intending to teach him a thing or two about common decency, Janette knocked on his door and waited a few seconds for a response. When one didn't come, she figured that if the music was blaring so loudly on her side of the door, it must be earsplitting on his. So, she banged on the wood that stood between her and serenity like she was a woman who had gotten a tip that her cheating boyfriend was on the other side of the door.

Finally, after Janette pounded for about a full three minutes, she could hear footsteps shuffling across the hardwood floor. Almost simultaneously, the deafening guitar solo came to an abrupt halt and the door swung open. Although Janette expected that he would answer at some point, which she hoped would be before her fist was black and blue, the sudden absence of the door caused her to lunge forward, directly into the arms of her musically antagonistic neighbor.

Floundering to regain both her balance and her composure, Janette looked up and for the first time noticed that her neighbor had beautiful light brown eyes rimmed with a tinge of hazel. She had never been this close to the man, nor had she ever planned to be, but she had to admit that she'd landed herself in worse positions with men who were far less attractive.

How did I overlook his handsome ruggedness the last time I had to come over here? she wondered to herself. *Because you were pissed off,* she remembered.

But before she could be distracted any further by her runaway thoughts and his good looks, he propped her into an upright position and wiped his hands on his pants as if to silently accuse her of being dirty. Yes, she was in a raggedy robe with sweats on underneath, but she wasn't dirty. Sweaty maybe, but not dirty.

His rude reaction reminded Janette that she was there to handle business, not to drool over this fine yet obviously ill-mannered specimen hindering her from a night of tranquility.

"I assume you're here … again … to complain about my music … again," he said with both a thick British accent and heavy annoyance in his tone.

"Well, my dad taught me that one should never assume because you'll make a you-know-what out of you and me," Janette shot back equally annoyed. "But, yes, here I am … again … to ask you … again … to turn your music down per our previous verbal agreement that you would do as such after 9:00 p.m."

"Do you always talk like that?" he asked while tilting his head to the side.

"Like what?" Janette asked as she mentally replayed her comment in slow motion.

"Like you're in a boardroom, courtroom, or some other kind of business setting," he replied.

Creasing her eyebrows while giving his question some consideration, Janette loosened up just a bit and responded, "I guess my brain must still be in work mode."

"What line of work are you in?" he asked while resting his shoulder against the door frame.

"Well, right now I'm a legal transcriptionist, but I have my sights set on being a criminal prosecutor. In fact, I'm studying for the bar exam." She wanted to add, "Which is why I need you to keep it down," but she stopped herself short.

"Oh! A beautiful woman with clear goals and the drive to match. I guess I'll give you a pass on all of the professional talk then," he said as his accent shone through once again.

Janette was so enamored by it that she almost overlooked him calling her beautiful. But when it sunk in, she felt her cheeks growing hot and immediately her lids started batting.

"Is there something caught in your eye?" he asked gruffly.

The way he went back and forth so quickly between rough and smooth threw Janette off a bit, but she disregarded his demeanor in order to stifle a giggle. Had he just mistaken instinctive flirting for her needing to rescue a stray, trapped eyelash?

I really need to work on that. But, if Todd had stuck around like he'd promised, I wouldn't have to.

Her thoughts trailed off as she felt her body ice over from the recollection of her horrible breakup with her ex. Refocusing her attention on her neighbor, Janette did her best to halt the memories of her past and "live in the now" like her therapist had often suggested.

Finally, she responded, "No, there's nothing in my eye. Thanks for asking."

"You're welcome," he replied. "So, Mrs. Lawyer. Can we renegotiate the terms of our agreement?" he asked.

"I'm actually not married, so Mrs. won't be necessary. My name is Janette."

"Ok, Janette. Nice to officially meet you," he said while extending his hand for her to shake. As she grasped it, he continued on with a twinkle in his eye and a slight upturn of his top lip. "Seems that we've never gotten around to introducing ourselves during any of your previous visits."

Janette noted that for the first time since he'd swung open his door, he had actually come close to smiling.

"It would seem that you're right about that," she responded while matching his playful tone. "And since you inquired so eloquently, I guess we can schedule a meeting to discuss amending our current verbal contract."

At that, they both laughed, having finally broken the ice.

"I'll keep it down for tonight," he told Janette. "And let's meet again soon to hash out the details. How does tomorrow at this time work for you?"

Janette had no idea what time it was or how long they'd been talking, but his charming accent and gentle eyes made it impossible for her to say no, so she nodded her head yes while trying not to seem excited. But, the truth was—this was as close as she'd come to a date in months.

As if reading her mind he said, "It's a date then. Tomorrow night at 10:30. Should I set up chairs here in the hallway or would you like to come inside?"

Janette couldn't help but smile. It was nice to know he had a sense of humor.

"I say we play it by ear," she responded with a wink.

The musical pun not lost on him, he winked back and said, "That sounds like music to my ears."

"And on that note," Janette said with a giggle as she turned to walk back to her door, "good night."

"Good night," he responded.

Janette heard his door close at the same time as hers. And as she made her way to the bathroom to brush her teeth and get ready for bed, she realized she'd never gotten his name.

Oh well, she thought giddily, *we'll get to that tomorrow.*

"You are altogether beautiful,
my love; there is no flaw in you."
—Song of Solomon 4:7

BUTT SIDE UP

As Candace rummaged through her purse to find her keys, she silently scolded herself for purchasing yet another high-priced designer bag that did nothing but make her blood boil when she had to fish things out of it. Plus, it was heavy from all the "necessities" she insisted on lugging around with her every day. No wonder her shoulder constantly hurt. Shaking her head as though she could see her own reflection, Candace said to herself, *Girl, you know you've got to do better. Your body is your temple. Remember?*

"Bring that sexy body over here and I'll do my best to take care of it for you," a low baritone voice responded from behind her.

The comeback threw Candace off for just a second because she hadn't realized that she was talking to herself out loud. But because she would recognize that voice in a sea of voices and she had the urge to play a little game of cat and mouse, she responded, "If you don't stop, I'll have to tell my husband you've been hitting on me again."

"I don't ever plan on stopping," the voice responded in an intense whisper.

Then, he spoke directly into her ear while pressing his frame against hers. Unable to ignore the sensation he was sending through her body, Candace dropped her purse to the ground and turned to embrace her husband, Jacob.

As she reached to wrap her arms around his neck, the moment was ruined by the extremely loud thud of her purse plummeting to the ground. What did she have in that thing, a ton of bricks?

The noisy and untimely distraction caused them to pause and remember where they were. As they looked at each other with sly grins, each confirmed what the other already knew—they couldn't very well make out on their doorstep. The retired neighbors in their uppity condo community would never stand for it. But what Candace and Jacob did behind closed doors was for them to know and their nosy neighbors never to find out, so they laughed while intending to move the action inside.

Jacob reached past Candace, who had still not located her keys, and opened their front door. He waited for her to walk inside, then he picked up her purse. With furrowed brows he wondered to himself, *What is my woman hauling around in this thing?* But, having grown up with a mother and two sisters, he knew never to question a woman about the contents of her precious pocketbook.

As soon as Jacob crossed the threshold of their bedroom and unloaded Candace's purse onto her favorite sky-blue velvet thinking chair, she pounced on him. By the way his body swayed, she realized that he was startled by her aggression, but it only took him a moment to steady himself and respond with equal force and passion. They kissed intensely while their body temperatures rose, and their clothes dropped to the plush carpeted floor. It had been far too long since they'd been able to get this close, so neither of them was going to hold back.

Wrapped in each other's arms, they fell backward onto the bed, whacking the ornate crystal lamp they had bought on one of their trips to Miami Beach. With a sharp crack, it toppled from the nightstand and shattered into a blizzard of broken crystals just inches from where they lay intertwined.

"Ouchhhhh!" Candace yelped, grabbing her right butt cheek in pain.

"Oh no, Sweetie, are you ok?" Jacob asked as he looked up at her.

But, from her scream and the tears that escaped her eyes and ran down her face, he already knew the answer. They had landed on the bed with Candace on top, and when the lamp collapsed onto the floor, a piece of the glass must have bounced up and got his wife good.

Dang it, Jacob thought, *I knew I shouldn't have put that thing so close to the bed!*

But he had no time to lament over his poor decision. Candace looked like she was in some serious pain. He had to take care of her.

He gently eased her off of him and as she lay on the bed, stomach down, he surveyed the damage. Jacob expected some squealing from Candace, who was usually an incredibly big baby when it came to cuts and scrapes, but instead he could hear her giggling into the pillow.

Without having to ask her what was so funny, Jacob let out a boisterous laugh. They both realized that it was inevitable that when Ms. Inez—a senior mother of the church who they'd welcomed into their home several years before—was out of the house for a few hours, something crazy would happen to them!

It was "Classic Jacob and Candace" to have a night of romance thwarted. Except this time, it was thwarted by a shard of glass to the butt.

THE SALT REMEDY

*Sometimes, when you least expect it,
faith finds its way to you.*

"Stupid wall!" Rebecca muttered as she banged against it.

Certain that she'd never get used to the new two-wheeled contraption that was now a permanent fixture in her life, she painstakingly continued down the long hallway. Nearing the elevator, panic rose as she wondered if she'd be able to press the button without tipping over. Thankfully (and from her perspective there hadn't been much to be thankful for lately) a man reached the elevator before she did and pressed the down button. Relief washed over her as the doors opened and no one was inside. She'd be able to get in without crushing anyone's toes.

Getting out might be another story, she thought to herself.

Three flights later with no new passengers—another rare "Thank God" occurrence—Rebecca exited the elevator and headed to the cafeteria. She wished she could have a stiff drink, but she was sure that was prohibited in the hospital. So, resentfully, she decided to try her hand at a strong cup of coffee.

"What can I do you for?" asked the lanky guy behind the Cup a Joe counter whose badge said Emmanuel.

Not sure what to order, Rebecca responded, "It's my first time. Do you have a special?"

"I've never seen you before, so I figured that," he responded with a slanted smile. "I'm bad with names, but I never forget a face."

Although his smile was inviting, Rebecca was nowhere close to being in the mood for a friendly conversation. Not after the news she'd just gotten from Dr. Roberts. But everyone didn't need to know how much life was sucking for her lately.

So, she threw on a fake smile and responded, "Yup, I'm new here and this'll be my first cup of coffee too."

"Whaaaaat?" he let out slowly as his eyes widened, "we get to be your first? I love that!"

Despite the cloud of doom hanging over Rebecca's head, she chuckled, her heart warmed by his cheerful response.

"To answer your question, our special today is the salted caramel latte. And trust me, we make it better than the other guys! But, since it's your first time, I guess you won't even be able to tell," he said with a warm smile. "Anyway, I'll have to give you the extra special!"

"And what's that?" Rebecca asked cautiously.

"No need to worry, My Lady. You just tell me if your favorite flavor is chocolate or vanilla and I'll whip something up for you. Don't worry, it's on the house. That way if you don't like it—no harm, no foul. But you're gonna love it!"

Rebecca found herself being drawn to Emmanuel's old school charm and even more so to his optimism. She needed as many doses of it as he could spare.

Feeling a smile rising on her face, she replied, "I know it's boring, but I'm a vanilla kinda gal."

"I'm a vanilla kinda guy myself, so I guess that makes us two boring peas in a pod," he responded with a wink.

As her cheeks grew hot, Rebecca bowed her head so that he couldn't see her blush. But when her lowered eyes caught sight of her legs hanging limp in what felt like her personal prison, her mind immediately grew cloudy.

Emmanuel's voice, laced with a concern Rebecca hadn't heard in years, sliced through her fog.

"Are you okay?" he asked.

His tender tone got the best of her, and tears gushed from her eyes before she could convince her brain to hold them back.

As if rushing into a fire to save lives, Emmanuel dashed from behind the counter and knelt next to Rebecca. To her surprise, he grabbed her hand gently in his and patted it.

"I'm no stranger to tears. I can even handle a little snot," Emmanuel said as he continued to console her. "After all, I do work in a hospital."

Although Rebecca hadn't known Emmanuel from Adam minutes prior, she was extremely thankful (there was that word again) for his support and his attempt to lighten her mood. Not wanting to make him feel bad for trying, Rebecca managed to crank out a tiny smile despite her torrential downpour of tears.

Suddenly conscious of the line of people waiting—far more patiently than Rebecca felt she deserved—Emmanuel stood and expertly guided her wheelchair toward a secluded table by the window.

"Don't you need to tell someone you'll be right back?" Rebecca asked between teary hiccups.

"No, they'll be just fine," he insisted as he pulled up a chair next to her and started patting her hand again.

Then, noticing her soft, persistent hiccups, he rushed away and came back with a glass of water.

"Here's some salt too," he said as he extended a teaspoon.

"Salt?" Rebecca paused, surprised, before taking the spoon.

"Yes, drink the water then follow it with a teaspoon of salt. It's an old trick. It'll work. Trust me."

Why would I trust a man I just met? Rebecca wondered.

But, strangely, she did. So, she tried it.

∞

They sat for a few minutes in silence while Rebecca attempted to gather her composure and Emmanuel prayed. He had seen and heard a lot during his short time at the hospital—from deaths to births and everything in between. The rollercoaster of sadness and joy had driven him to his knees more times than he could count.

"Sounds like your hiccups stopped," Emmanuel said, breaking the quiet that hung between them. "I used to have them almost every day when I was little, so my mom was thankful when my grandmother passed down the salt remedy."

Ever since Rebecca could remember, she had gotten the hiccups every time she cried too hard, like now. But, still too emotional to speak and let Emmanuel know they had that in common too, she just nodded her head to confirm that her hiccups were gone.

Sensing that she wasn't ready to talk about the challenge she was facing, he continued with his one-sided conversation.

"Did you know that if you pour salt on concrete it will help to keep you from slipping on snow or ice? It also works wonders on dirty pots and pans. And my favorite use for it is making Play-Doh!"

Appreciative of the light conversation that kept her from having to reveal why she had broken down crying, Rebecca finally piped in.

"Really? I didn't know about the Play-Doh one. Did you know you can also use it to help clean up raw eggs if you drop them on your kitchen floor?"

Emmanuel's eyebrows shot up like she was telling him the secret to the fountain of youth, so she continued.

"Yup. Just pour salt over the eggs and wait two minutes before wiping them up. And voila!"

"Isn't it a wonder how much we can do with such a small element?" Emmanuel asked sounding awestruck.

"You're right," Rebecca responded while nodding. "If God exists, He certainly made a big purpose for it."

As soon as the words left her mouth, she regretted them. What did she mean "If"? She had to admit though that since Dr. Roberts had given her the diagnosis, she'd examined her belief in God and wasn't so sure anymore.

Emmanuel started to speak, then stopped. Rebecca longed for his reply, but not wanting to force it, she let the silence settle in once again.

A few minutes later, his eyes met hers and he said, "Even though I'm not good at names, I'd love to know yours."

Rebecca had expected Emmanuel to have a retort—or at the very least question her "If God exists" statement—but she was relieved he hadn't. Religion could get touchy for people who had known each other for years, much less minutes. It did leave her unsure what that meant about his relationship with God though. But she had bigger issues and no energy to delve into his spiritual life.

"My name is Rebecca," she responded.

"Well, I'm sure you've realized by now that my name is Emmanuel," he said while pointing to his badge. "So, tell me something, Rebecca," he continued, "where does love come from?"

He studied her as she gulped in air, bracing himself for one of the standard retorts he had heard from non-Christians (and even atheists) in the very same cafeteria in which they now sat. He did his best to maintain the tenderness in his eyes. The last thing he wanted to do was make Rebecca defensive and possibly lose the chance to share his faith with her.

Once again, Rebecca locked eyes with Emmanuel. Not sure how to respond just yet, she raised the glass of water to her lips, took a sip, then placed it gently back on the table.

After a few more moments, she let out a long, deep breath and spoke thoughtfully as her voice quivered.

"Honestly, I feel like I don't know anymore. Just twenty-four hours ago, I would have had the perfect answer to that question. One that would never cause anyone to have even the slightest doubt that I was a Christian through and through. But today … uhm … I'm just not sure …"

Her voice hitched, each word catching in her throat, as her shoulders sank like broken wings and her head dipped in silent resignation.

"I've lost my hope and now I'm afraid that my faith is about to follow. I guess I still believe God exists, I'm just not sure if He cares about or loves me," Rebecca admitted as her eyes fell downward.

Following her gaze, Emmanuel looked from her legs back to her face. He had seen people's faith in crisis before, but he felt something especially deep for Rebecca.

"I know that when my faith wavers and I'm going through what feels like a mountain of doubt, hurt, and pain, I don't feel like praying. But I've realized that that's exactly when I need to pray the most. So, do you mind if we pray together right now?"

There was nothing in Rebecca that felt like praying, but she knew Emmanuel was right. This was exactly the time she needed to pray the most, so she held out her hands. And as Emmanuel took them in his and they bowed their heads, she felt more peace than she'd felt in a long time.

His voice bursting with passion and sincerity, Emmanuel prayed, "Father God, we know that you sent Jesus to die on the cross for our sins and our sicknesses, so we come to You humbly and give You our hurting hearts. You are our good Father. We trust You. So, we ask that You give us the faith we need for the trials we are facing. I lift up your daughter, Rebecca, to you right now and I ask that you give her a peace that surpasses all understanding. Thank you for loving us and for putting us here to, like salt, season this world with your love! Help us to do just that. In Jesus' name we pray. Amen."

"You are the salt of the earth."
—Matthew 5:13

ABOUT THE AUTHOR

Ty Scott King is an internationally known poet, rapper, speaker, and bestselling author. She is also a proud wife, daughter, sister, auntie, and friend. Founder of R.I.S.E. Up Arts Initiative, Ty is cultivating a global platform for faith-based poetry and music while empowering young creatives to explore their own potential.

Often hailed as the "Maya Angelou of this generation," she has shared stages with industry legends, mesmerized international audiences, and even graced the prestigious halls of the United States Pentagon with her artistry.

Ty has been featured in national radio ads for corporate giants like McDonald's (earning a coveted Silver Mic Award), Pizza Hut, and Aveeno. Television viewers have witnessed her talent on major networks like BET,

TBN, and TV One. Her music has enjoyed multiple long runs on the Billboard charts and her poetry has garnered GRAMMY® Award consideration.

Ty's messages resonate deeply, reminding a world-wide audience of their inherent worth and purpose. *Doses: Love & Friendship in Vibrant Pieces* is her fourth published book.

Learn more at www.tyscottking.com